# SHUT

# UP

# AND

# DANCE

## TANZANIA GLOVER

Cover Art by Aaronya Medici

www.tanzaniaglover.com

Booking With Love
332 S Michigan Ave

**TANZANIA GLOVER**

Suite #121- 2217
Chicago, IL 60604
www.bookingwithlove.com

To my beautiful mother,
I miss your hugs and kisses more
than life, but the one thing I won't
ever have to miss is your love
because I can still feel it wrapped
around me every single day.
It's still San & Tan forever.

∞

# 1
## DANCING WITH A STRANGER

My stomach was full and my balls were freshly drained. According to the laws of manhood I didn't have much to be complaining about at the moment, but a nigga like me always could find something if I wanted to because I wasn't happy.

And I hadn't been for a while.

Twenty-five was far from ancient, but it seemed like ever since hitting that milestone last year I wanted something more out of life.

Something new.

Something different.

"Theo, get up! I can't find my bra," Nat complained as she tossed around the pillows that we had just tossed aside to make room for us on the bed.

After the car accident I had outright refused to get the bulky ass hospital bed that the doctors recommended for me because my California King always made me feel like one. Instead my mama had just brought over more pillows than the law should allow as a compromise since I really did have to keep my head and feet elevated while I recovered.

I had healed up better than anybody expected and fast too so I could have gotten rid of them by now, but I guess I had gotten used to rolling over and feeling like somebody was there with me again since Nat rarely was.

She had given me plenty of head to help with the healing, but as soon as I was back up and walking again so was she.

"What you need it for anyway?" I yawned out about her little ass titties before she hit the back of my head with one of the bigger pillows.

"You need to be helping me look for it before one of your hoes finds it," she spat since she swore I was knocking down everything in LA but the palm trees when it couldn't be further from the truth.

It was actually just a few here and there and it would've been none if she just admitted that she wanted to be with me again.

"Nah. You know you're the only hoe I bring in here," I said sounding serious then ducked when I saw her getting ready to hit me again. "Bae stop. I'm playing."

I took my time stretching and rolling over because I had been felt the underwire underneath me. I just wanted her to stay until I went to rehearsal later, but I didn't exactly want to come right out and ask her to.

For over two years now I had been trying to get us back on track, but nothing I did seemed to work. It was funny though because even though she claimed not to want a relationship with me, she seemed to only stop by to fuck then feed me just often enough to keep me from finding something real with somebody else.

Our present situation had stopped satisfying me at least a year ago, but I kept allowing it because I just wanted any piece of her that I could get my hands on. Well that and a part of me was proud of the fact that she still hadn't found somebody that could do it like me.

I couldn't put all the blame on her for where we stood though since we had both did our share of straying over the years. And truthfully the main reason we always found ourselves right back where we started was because the sexual chemistry we had was off the charts.

But it didn't mean much anymore without the connection that we used to have. I would have taken that over everything too because I couldn't ever really see myself getting it from somebody else. And no it didn't hurt that she looked like a model except she had a little more ass, but even if she didn't I wasn't like a lot of these niggas out here. I put loyalty over everything and no matter what I would always still rather be with my day one.

Still I had been warning her for a while now to either piss or get off the pot, but she didn't believe me. And I guess she had no reason to since I never followed through before.

"Hold up. You still coming to my show tomorrow, right?" I asked after realizing that she was already fully dressed and about to walk out without saying goodbye.

"I thought I told you I had to work."

"Ask Neek to do it for you," I suggested because getting her little sister to fill in was her go to whenever she wanted to do hoe shit with her friends.

"Mm mn. Nobody is trying to get a headache from your screaming ass fans anyway. I might come by after if I'm not tired," she said throwing me a bone that I happily caught because something was better than nothing even though if it were her I would've just put on a smile and some ear plugs.

But I had learned a long time

ago to stop expecting me out of other people. I still needed the reminder every now and then though.

There was no way I would ever be able to prove it, but I did have a theory that she loved me more when I didn't have shit but a couple dollars and a dream to my name. Back then if I couldn't count on shit else, I knew my rent would be due and I knew my baby would be front and center at any hole in the wall spot that would let me perform.

Her plus was her minus though because I did generally love that she never treated me any differently based on the size of my deposit slips. To her I would always just be the same dusty nigga that used to borrow her car to go to the studio while she had class.

I knew everybody thought that she was too good for me then and that I was just chasing a pipe dream, but as luck would have it she didn't even use her degree and had ended up working in her pop's sneaker store. Meanwhile I was cashing out every time I pulled out my pen to write a new love song.

I guess her life not going how she planned so far had soured her up some, but ultimately I knew that nothing had changed her for the worse more than losing our baby boy a few years ago. Neither one of us was ready for a kid at the time so it was probably for the best, but it sure as hell didn't feel like that then...or even now.

We went from picking out names and cribs to a casket and deciding if an obituary was even necessary for a stillborn. It wasn't and honestly just looking at the only picture we had of him on one made shit even harder than it had to be.

And even though his death was nobody's fault, I still felt responsible for filling that hole in her heart that had been caused by our loss. And more than anything

I wanted to be the one to bring back the old Natalie Carter then finally turn her into Natalie Smith…at least that's what I used to want.

I didn't want to dwell on that all day though so I pushed Nat and all that came with her to the back of my mind when I got up to shower. I turned my phone off whenever I was with her so when I powered it back on for a playlist I expected a few missed calls, but not the fifty-two that I saw. My frown instantly turned upside down because I knew what it meant.

I officially had my first number one single.

My manager Jonathan confirmed it by popping the cork on a bottle of champagne as soon as he answered my FaceTime call.

"Ay you heard back from ol' girl about the video yet?" I asked about the dancer that had made the viral video that led to all of this.

Since hers first popped up a few weeks ago thousands had followed doing and attempting to do her original choreography. All of that traffic had driven a song that I had to fight my label to even include on the album all the way up the charts.

I hated that shit like this and not just raw talent was what the music industry had become, but I wouldn't complain about it now because it was finally working in my favor. I had been singing my heart out, writing the best songs, dancing til I dropped while playing the drums, keys, bass and guitar.

I was like talent personified, but it had barely gotten me on the world's radar until Tempest Randall's fine ass decided to shake hers to my song.

She got an instant follow back on social media the first time I saw it. And I didn't know why I was surprised to see that she was already following me since she had danced to my song after all.

Usually I wouldn't follow women, not even fans, out of respect for Nat, but I was finally feeling tired of sparing her feelings when she didn't bother doing the same for me.

"Right. I knew it was something I forgot to do," he said about contacting Tempest as he unconvincingly snapped his fingers out of frustration. "But I already had another chick in mind anyway and shorty is baaad," he emphasized. "We can just send your girl flowers and an autograph. She'll love it."

Off top I could tell he was lying to me because that was the only time he started speaking a mile per minute. I knew exactly what I wanted to say to him, but I thought it over for a couple seconds because Jonathan had been like family since before even becoming my manager.

"J, be real with me. You set a reminder for everything and your phone stays glued to your hand. So if you forgot that means you didn't write it down and if you didn't write it down it's because you knew you weren't gonna do it in the first place."

I kept my voice calm because I didn't want confrontation during what was supposed to be a moment of celebration, but I knew if he didn't start telling me what I wanted to hear and soon then my volume control would be the least of his worries.

He let out a deep sigh like he had something important to say, but it was just more bullshit and theatrics. "Alright I'mma level with you. No this ain't your first video, but it's definitely about to be your introduction to the world so the visuals are just as important as the music. Now the girl you want is *cute for a big girl*, mad talented, all of that, right? But we need somebody that's gonna take this to the next level and she ain't it."

"Wait so you don't want her in the video because she's a 'big girl'?" I asked with quote fingers. "Nigga *you're* a big girl," I reminded him since he had been eating good off of me for years.

And it wasn't like I hadn't noticed that she didn't look like the average video girl. It just wasn't an issue. If you had it then you just had it. And she had it. All of it and then some.

"Now stop fucking around and get her. She's already probably about to run my pockets for asking so late anyway."

"Alright. You got it. But don't say you weren't warned when she takes up the whole damn screen," he barely got out because he was too busy laughing at his own joke, but I saw my face remain stoic in the corner of my screen.

I didn't know if I was just still in a funk because of Nat, but I didn't find anything funny about the disrespect and weird energy he seemed to have about her.

"You know you of all people need to be thanking Tempest for doing your job better than you. How long have you been trying to get me on the charts let alone at the top?" I asked rhetorically because we had just celebrated five years of working together recently.

"Exactly. **I want her**, J," I finally admitted it to myself even though I hoped he didn't pick up on just how many ways I meant it. "So do your thing and make it happen."

"Why don't you go get your dancing queen yourself then since you sound so passionate about her?" he asked still sounding amused with himself.

"You know that's actually not a bad idea. If you want something done right, you gotta do it yourself."

After ending the call I was just as frustrated as I had been before Nat left so I did the only thing that had been putting me in a better mood these days. I put on Tempest's video.

It had millions of views now

and I was personally responsible for more than I would've liked to admit. But with her smooth skin that looked like the blackest of midnights and those long cinnamon colored locs that teasingly tickled the top of her butt when she danced, I couldn't tear my eyes away.

I'd just came not that long ago, but my dick was already rising to the occasion again just from watching the ripple effect of the thick flesh on her ass. That shit was mesmerizing and even weeks later I still couldn't get enough of it. If she could do *any* of that on my dick I knew I would be hooked instantly.

A few views later and after double tapping her latest Instagram posts, I finally got in the shower and washed off the scent of Nat while letting my mind wonder if I would ever get to find out what it was like to be covered in the scent of Tempest.

# 2
## SHALL WE DANCE

There was a lot riding on tonight's show so I wanted-- no I needed everything to go as planned. Before my label was willing to commit to investing in my first arena tour, they wanted to make sure I was back up to it physically again after the accident. And there was no better way for them to determine that than watching me do what I did best.

Thanks to the single and a gang of popular supporting acts I had sold out the Staples Center, something I thought would easily take me another few years to do. Ten thousand souls would be in their seats waiting for me to show them a good time, but even with all of that pressure I wasn't nervous at all.

I had been rehearsing for just under a month so I hit every mark effortlessly and my vocals had never been better. More than that though I had another reason to be confident.

Tempest was coming.

At least she was *supposed* to be coming. I knew exactly where she should've been sitting because I always had spare tickets to give away to fans last minute if Nat or my parents didn't want to watch from the crowd. From the side of the stage I combed the front row with my eyes for the fourth time. She still wasn't there yet and I was on next.

"DeeDee, are you sure she got the tickets? Let me see what she said again," I asked reaching for my little sister's phone. I wasn't supposed to know the code, but she always made it consecutive numbers so it was easy to crack.

Nat was uncomfortable with every single other assistant I'd had for one reason or another so I eventually just gave the job to DeeDee to give her something to do. She treated me like an ATM anyway so it made sense to put her to work and keep her little wild ass out of trouble.

"Boy if you don't give me my phone! Get pussy off the brain and go get dressed already."

She pushed me out of her way and towards my dressing room, but I knew it was just because she liked the group that I had as one of my supporting acts for the night. I shook my head at how sprung she looked off the corny grinding that they were doing on stage.

"You know I really regret

begging for a little sister sometimes."

"Yeah and sometimes I regret missing out on college to schedule your fuck sessions," she said before jokingly flipping me off. "And since when do you fuck with fat girls anyway? Is this some kind of Oedipal thing because I always knew there was some weird shit between you and Mama?"

"First off I'm definitely telling Ma you called her fat. And how am I Oedipus when you're the one always talking about how you want a dude like Pops?" I challenged her before running back to my dressing room when I realized that the group was finally done humping the speakers.

The lights were low when I ascended from below the stage, but when they came back on Tempest's was the first face I noticed in the crowd, front and center. From jump I was excited at the way her jean shorts and thigh high boots fit, but when I saw that she was wearing a tour shirt with my face on it I knew this was about to be one helluva night.

I began the show by playing my guitar right in front of her, strumming on it like I had been dreaming of doing to her body since I first laid eyes on it. I couldn't help but watch her off and on throughout my set to see if she was enjoying herself. After a few songs it was clear that she definitely was though.

She sang along to all the words and even put on a show of her own dancing with her friend. She twerked to an older up-tempo song of mine and blew a big ignorant bubble with the wad of pink gum in her mouth. She danced like nobody was watching even though anybody who was near wouldn't be able to look away. Her entire row and a few behind her weren't even paying attention to me because they were too busy cheering her on.

That's when the best idea I'd had in a while popped in my head. But first I had to get eyes back on me so I finally relieved myself of my shirt. I had long given up my membership to the club for the bird chested niggas, but not being able to work out and eating so much during my recovery time had filled me out even more. Now it wasn't just my young fans lusting after me. I finally had the attention of the grown ass women that I always wanted.

I usually just threw shirts as far into the crowd as I could without caring where it ended up, but this time I practically handed it right to Tempest. She didn't have it for long though, I saw as I watched her give it to a teenaged girl next to her that had been screaming her face off for me all night. It was cool because I definitely had something else I wanted to give her even more.

My set started winding down and right on schedule Tempest's dance video began playing on all the big screens in the background. The entire crowd went wild and I couldn't help but smile as she excitedly jumped up and down for herself up there since she only had calm and confident energy for me all night.

"You know I love all y'all,

right?" I asked into the mic and was met with more screams.

"But this woman right here…" I began then stopped to admire my favorite part where she hit the perfect split. "She helped me get my first number one record today. I invited her here tonight to say thank you, but it still doesn't really feel like enough. So how do y'all think I should thank her?"

Tempest was still in shock and watching herself, but I laughed out loud when I heard some fans screaming to pay her and others saying things that had already crossed my mind more than a time or two.

"You know what? How about I just bring her up here and ask her directly?" I said which had been the plan all along, but I saw her suddenly get nervous which made me wonder if putting her on the spot like that was the wrong thing to do.

It was too late to turn back now though especially since I knew I wasn't letting her leave here without at least attempting to shoot my shot.

"I know you're not scared?" I asked her in a challenging tone as I squatted down to be closer to her. "You've been down there teasing me and trying to get my attention all night. Well you got it

now so what you gon' do with it?"
I dared her and that was all it took
for her to remove her fanny pack
and hand it to her friend.

Instead of waiting for her to
take the seat that had been
brought out for her, I sat down
because I could already sense that
she wouldn't just sit there and let
me sing to her after what I had
said. And when I saw her securing
her long high ponytail and
adjusting her boots, I knew I was
about to experience something
different.

As she approached me I
noticed that she wasn't as tall as
she seemed in her videos, still a
stallion through and through

though and those thick legs went on for days. I couldn't stay focused on them for as long as I wanted to though since I almost forgot where I was for a minute once her big brown eyes were peering down from right in front of me.

There were thousands of people behind her shouting my name, but the only sound I could hear was her raspy voice as she bent to speak to me for the first time.

"You can thank me by putting your hands behind your back," she ordered with authority showing that she was familiar with this part of my show. I did as

I was told and let her place the handcuffs on me when one of my backup dancers brought them out.

From the top down nobody on my team liked surprises so I wasn't surprised when I saw a stageside Jonathan on pins and needles waiting to shut it all down. I nodded for him to just let it happen as I got comfortable and gave her enough room to sit it on my lap if she felt inclined to.

The live band behind me had been playing along the whole time, but luckily somebody had acted fast enough to drop the track as soon as she put a golden arch in her back so deep that

McDonald's would've been proud.

Her body already looked like it was made for sex, but bent over with all of that close enough to kiss nearly sent me into overdrive. Thick was an understatement. She had more dips and curves than a California highway and the sensual style of dancing that she started doing made them even more dangerous. Fuck it that shit was lethal.

I just knew a boot would slip and kick me in the face with all of her moves on the floor, but she was an expert and kept it sexy and safe as she freakily freestyled for me. And she didn't just swing her hair around haphazardly either. She used the long locs like an accessory and made them dance alongside her body.

It was sexy as fuck how she made them smack her ass when she whipped her head back. And when she danced next to me it was like they were reaching out and touching me. It ignited something in me and made me glad that I had all of my shows professionally filmed. I mean I was still experiencing it, but I couldn't wait to watch the footage back and have this forever.

*You got more than your average*
*That's why you could never be*
*average*

I took in my lyrics for the first time in a while as they blasted through the arena speakers. I had written the song last year before I ever knew she existed, but I guess I had unintentionally written them for a woman just like her anyway.

The song was finally coming to a close, but it looked like she planned on finishing strong as she circled me like a vulture then ran her hands over my face and bare chest. I almost broke my damn neck trying to see what she was doing back there because it felt like she was pulling something animalistic out of me.

When she was in my line of sight again I instinctively reached out to grab her only to be reminded that my hands were still stuck behind me. It turned out to be a good thing too because by that point they had a mind of their own and would have been all over her otherwise.

But even though I couldn't touch her, it didn't stop her from touching me and it definitely didn't stop my body from responding to her as she finally entered the danger zone. Usually I could control south of the border with no problem, but grinding on me to the beat how she did was overkill and it made me as stiff as stone. I knew a million eyes and cameras were on me so I tucked in my lip trying to hide how much more I wanted her to do to me.

When she eventually felt the consequences of her actions she brought her hips to a full stop then looked at me with a coy smile, clearly pleased that she had that kind of effect on me. I wasn't apologizing for it either because I didn't know a man or woman alive that could have survived what I'd just been through without coming out turned on.

"*That's* what it looks like when I'm trying to get somebody's attention, Theo," she said cockily before blowing a bubble in my face. In playful retaliation I popped it with my teeth then stole the gum from her as she giggled like a kid. "Hey! That was my last piece!"

"Here. Take it back then," I dared her as I chewed on the almost flavorless gum trying to decipher what she tasted like.

She just continued laughing at me while shaking her head in defiance as the crowd chanted for her to take it back. I thanked God for peer pressure because after a minute she closed her eyes and quickly grabbed it from me but not before I could swipe her juicy bottom lip with my tongue first.

It sounded like the arena was

roaring by that point, but I never could understand why the women in the crowd enjoyed these parts of the show so much. I remembered being jealous watching Janet Jackson turn men into fools on stage because I'd wanted it to be me.

I had gotten even more than I bargained for out of Tempest though, I thought as I noticed that she'd even lost both of her big hoop earrings doing shit to me that would make Janet blush.

From behind I felt somebody unlocking my hands from the cuffs, but I didn't bother glancing back to see who it was because I was more focused on the gourmet meal still seated on my lap.

"Alright that's my time. Y'all be safe out there," I joked when I was finally free then pretended that I was leaving with Tempest.

When I stood with her legs still wrapped around me I could see that even she looked surprised that I could carry her so easily. I took my time letting her down though because I had been dreaming of having her that close to me for weeks now albeit with a little more privacy and less clothes.

She thanked me for being a good sport then took a silly bow to the crowd before trying to get back down to her seat. I immediately put a stop to that and instead directed her backstage because I wasn't about to let that be the end of our first meeting.

When she was out of sight I got back to my regular set and ended things on a high note and it was probably because I felt more confident knowing who I had watching me from the side now. When I got backstage I saw that she was surrounded by a bunch of people including her friend who I had seen escorted out after I started the last song.

Tempest was basking in all of the attention and I couldn't help but smile at how I was almost being ignored like I wasn't the damn headliner. But even I had to admit that she had stolen the show in the best way possible.

She must have felt me watching her because she suddenly turned in my direction and returned my smile then waved. I motioned for her to do her thing for a little bit longer while I got changed and she nodded.

The second I was alone I jumped out of the hot ass leather pants I was wearing then took a quick shower because I didn't want to keep her waiting on me for too long. By the time I made it out I was worried that she had left because I didn't see her after getting stopped by a couple people from the label. I relaxed though when I noticed her seated and looking comfortable like she had planned on staying as long as it took to see me again.

She still wasn't by herself though and I silently cursed myself for not really thinking this whole thing through. After all we had just done I wanted to get to talk to her one on one, but I knew I couldn't just invite her back to the hotel without offending her. I would have for sure kept it PG if she preferred though because I did honestly want to feel her out some before *feeling her out some*.

"Thanks for coming out tonight, Temp," I said attempting to sound more familiar than I actually was with her as I copped a seat across from her.

"Thank you for inviting me. My original seats were up in the nosebleeds because I missed the presale."

"Oh so you were already coming to see me then?" I asked sounding a little full of myself which made her grin.

"I definitely was. You're always doing those big festivals, but I don't do drunk white people or heat so I have to wait around for civilized shows like this."

"Well I appreciate it. And I

meant what I said out there. I gotta find a way to thank you for real," I said getting ready to bring up my video, but she interrupted me before I could spit it out.

"I mean if you insist…you got Birkin money yet?" she cracked as she reached out and playfully patted my pockets.

"I'll go find some if that's what you want," I said in all seriousness even though I thought those things were a waste of money.

"Perfect response but no. How about instead you give your biggest fan the full version of some of those snippets you're always teasing us with? You got me ripping them off your IG lives and YouTube like I'm a peasant," she said causing me to chuckle at her silliness.

"Bet, but I know you're not talking about teasing niggas. You ain't have to do all of that when you knew I had a show to close out. I almost forgot some of the lyrics," I exaggerated just to gas her up some more.

"Sorry. On-stage Tempest cannot be contained. Sis be getting me into so much trouble out here."

"I could see that," I said playing along like she actually had two identities. "So what you and her about to get into?" I asked sounding more forward than I wanted to, but I wanted to know.

"Probably just grab something to eat then drop my girl off," she said casually and we both looked over at her friend like we remembered that we weren't alone at the same time. She had been awake just a minute ago, but she was sleeping soundly amongst the backstage chaos now.

"Why wassup? 'Cause if you're going to the studio then we can twerk sum' while you write new songs," she offered playfully and I noticed how contagious her smile was. "Oh before I forget, can I get a picture please?"

"What kind you want? Silly or sexy?"

"Um hello. Both," she said like it should have been obvious as she patted the seat beside her. I sat close enough to get a nose full of her intoxicating perfume again only now it was mixed with my cologne and I appreciated the blend even more.

I humored her and let her take as many pictures as she wanted until she was satisfied then asked her to send me a couple to share too. That's when I knew she wasn't exaggerating about being a huge fan of mine because her eyes lit up like a Christmas tree at just the thought of me posting her.

I wanted to get her out of the fan-zone though and fast because I definitely didn't look at her the way I looked at the rest of my fans.

"It was nice finally meeting you," I told her as I opened my arms for a hug then thought about how to go about smoothly asking for her number because I honestly couldn't even remember the last time I had done that.

"Same. I just knew you would be an asshole because your songs are so sweet, but you really are like a real life little choirboy," she said looking up at me like I was a God or something.

"Nah I'm far from that. Actually," I began but was cut off by the sound of Nat's voice from behind us.

"There you are. I've been looking all over for you," she said before dropping her bag off in the seat I had just been in. She was still dressed in her Kickzone polo, but I could tell that she had put on fresh makeup just for me. She looked good.

"Wassup? You were back here the whole time?" I asked before noticing I was too close to Tempest to see how she received Nat's sudden appearance.

"Just the last few songs, but you did so good. You always do good," she said before planting a big kiss on my cheek and it wasn't lost on me that her arms found their way around me for an embrace too.

She must've definitely seen or at least heard about how me and Tempest had just cut up on stage. By the time she released me she still hadn't acknowledged Tempest so I did the honors and introduced them.

"Oh hey. You did good too. I might have to come take a pole-dancing class or two with you." Nat's tone came across complimentary, but anybody would have been a fool to think there was anything but malice coating every word that fell from her pretty mouth.

"Thanks, but we actually don't have any poles where I work. You would still for sure enjoy yourself though because we do get wild on Fridays," Tempest said extending a genuine invitation.

While they talked and made plans that I knew Nat wouldn't keep, I looked around backstage at all the women that had come out hoping to get a chance with me or any of the other artists and their entourages. I had to admit that there was a decent lineup of eights, nines and tens, but I couldn't help but notice how much they all looked alike. Literally the same girl with slight variations. Nat too.

I felt like I was trying to find Waldo for a while until I remembered the one who stood out without even trying.

"Ay Temp, y'all want to roll with me to get something to eat?" I asked interrupting Nat because we would've been there all night with how interested she was pretending to be in Tempest's work as a dancer and choreographer.

I didn't mean to be so rude, but she was kind of asking for it since I couldn't remember the last time she had been all on me like that.

"Mm no it's getting late and I really should be getting her home even though I highly doubt she'll be going to work in the morning," she remarked as she woke her friend up and they started preparing to leave.

"Alright well thanks again for everything and I'mma have my sister send you that stuff, okay?" I promised as I slid an arm back around her waist in a half-hug before she could get up.

"Okay and do it soon please because me and Patience ain't never been friends," she joked before saying goodbye to both of us.

Forgetting that Nat was still beside me, I watched Tempest walk away from me until she turned a corner. The only thing that wiped the dumb smile from my face was Nat barely letting her get out of earshot before she was questioning me about what I would send her.

"Mind your business," I told her in an even tone as I finally got up to get my stuff because both hunger and sleepiness were creeping up on me.

"So you're not my business now?"

"I don't know. Am I?" I flipped the question on her since our limbo status had been completely on her for the last couple years.

"Whatever. I didn't come here to argue."

"So what did you come for?"

"Because you asked me to," she said simply and I couldn't argue with that because I had. A lot had already changed since yesterday though and I told myself I wouldn't make that mistake again.

I ended my night in a lush hotel bed with not nearly as many pillows as I was used to now. The fact that a lightly snoring Nat laid next to me should have made up for them, but it didn't and I tossed and turned while my mind raced and replayed my night.

I licked my lips, savoring the brief contact that they had experienced with Tempest's just hours ago. I exhaled in frustration because I wished that I would have been bold enough to go after who I really wanted to be sleeping next to for the night. There was still a slight chance for me to get it right though.

On the ride here I'd remembered that with all that was going on backstage I completely forgot to bring up the video to Tempest. Of course I could've had DeeDee contact her like before or even done it myself this time, but I would've used any and every excuse to get to see her again.

I had overheard her giving Nat directions to her downtown LA dance studio, but I also saw the location on a few of the videos that I watched after going to the bathroom in the middle of the night for some privacy. Seeing her had me feeling like I was back on stage again then thinking about how long ago it'd been since I'd been this excited over somebody so quickly.

And I mean I *loved* being in love. I straight craved that shit because there was nothing like exchanging energy and loving on somebody who loved you back.

But this toxic shit with Nat had me all out of my element. For months all I could write about were the hard parts of relationships and even though the songs sounded good the topic was already old and stale to me.

I wanted to sing about real love again.

But I would definitely need a new muse for that kind of new music and for really no discernable reason at all, I kind of got the feeling that I might've just stumbled across the right woman for the job.

# 3
# MAY I HAVE THIS DANCE

Looking forward to the weekend was a luxury I hadn't experienced in a long time. And since I had spent the better part of the first quarter stuck on my back just about anything was better than that, but this specific weekend would be special for a different reason.

I had kept my distance from Tempest since the concert almost a week ago, but not seeing her hadn't stopped me from thinking about her all the time. I officially knew it was going a little bit passed just crushing status though when I found myself overthinking what I would wear when I pulled up on her Friday night dance class. I wanted to be comfortable, but I wanted her to see my dick print too so I purposely went with the classic grey sweats and a shorter t-shirt.

Nat had been blowing me up all day because it was about that time, but I ignored her calls since I planned on saving all my energy potentially for Tempest. Just thinking about being in the same room as her again had me geeked as I double checked to make sure I had everything.

As I was headed out the door I ran right into Nat pulling in next to my car in the driveway. See this was the shit that I was talking about. She wanted girlfriend privileges like being able to pop up unannounced without the title and other expectations, but that shit was not about to fly today. I wasn't letting anything, not Nat or traffic, stop me from getting across town tonight.

"Where you going looking like a thot?" she asked when she saw that her presence didn't stop me from unlocking my car and throwing my bag in the back seat.

"Pole-dancing," I said sarcastically knowing she would catch on that I was on the way to see Tempest.

"With that little--well actually that *big* fan of yours?" she asked taking a shot at Tempest and I almost smiled when I caught it. "She's been around a lot lately."

She was referring to our second viral moment when a fan shared the video of Tempest acting up at my concert. I knew she had seen it because she never brought it up which only made it even more obvious that it bothered her.

"Yeah a lil' bit. I'm about to go ask her to do the video," I told her hoping to end the conversation as I hopped in the driver's seat, but she held me up when she caught the door and stopped it from closing.

"Now you're putting her in your video? Let me find out that's lowkey *you* or something," she said with a funny tone that I didn't like.

I knew it had to be about her weight, but it was a subject she should have been on mute about because weight or no weight Tempest was badder in every way possible. And her current attitude, crossed arms and screwface only made what I was about to do much easier too.

"You know actually that is *all me*," I said getting a little ahead of myself. "Or at least she will be by the time you see the video. And I can already tell that my new girl will be territorial so this is probably the last time you should be showing up like this."

"Theo please. You're the one who's always calling and begging me to stay over so let's not even go there."

"You're right, but I guess you don't gotta worry about that no more now. This shit been ran its course anyway."

"We'll see. Go frolic with

your big bitch and don't come running back to me when it's over."

"Aw now don't be actin' salty because she got your meal ticket," I said knowing it would piss her off because even when I did finally get some money she honestly was never really too concerned with it.

"Oh sis definitely got some meals," she cracked again.

"Yup and about to get some more. Get your weight up, lil' booty," I teased her as I finally shut the door then pulled off. All I saw in my rearview were two stiff, childish middle fingers.

I didn't know if what I had

just said about me and Tempest was true or not, but I really didn't like all the negativity that was being thrown at her for no reason. Literally all she seemed to want to do was shake her ass and have fun, but she was already being judged by people who didn't even know her. I sighed hard thinking about how now I really could use some dancing to help clear my head.

I wasn't surprised to see that the class was sold out when I went to check in, but the woman behind the front desk recognized me and told me to hurry up and slide in before it started. She almost forgot to make me pay, but I was already a step ahead of her because I wanted Tempest to get all of her money.

I smiled to myself when I saw that her prices had gone up since all the recent exposure because I'd remembered thinking she was literally selling herself short when I looked them up before.

I had planned on getting there early to get some private face time in with her before class started, but I was running late because since the accident I had been driving like Miss Daisy was in the back seat. I tried to quietly open the door to avoid interrupting anything, but it was a waste of time because the second I stepped inside all eyes were on me.

Tempest was already wearing a big smile before she stopped speaking, but it almost doubled in size along with her eyes when she realized it was me underneath the hoodie. I saw her try to hide it, but it was too late. She was happy to see me too.

"Oop! Looks like young Theodore came back for seconds, Tempest," a flamboyant man said from the back of class and everybody laughed.

He wasn't wrong about anything he'd said, but I hated it when people reminded me that I had a young face. I had already assumed she was a few years older than me, but now I knew I would have to ask about it when we were alone again.

Without a word the class parted like the Red Sea as she walked through them towards me. I didn't even bother with a greeting and instead just reached out for the hug I wanted. I could tell she hesitated because of all the eyes on us, but I liked that she brushed them off and stepped into it anyway since we both knew she wanted it too.

My arms naturally went around her waist and it took everything in me not to grab a handful of ass after seeing how it looked in the mirror in front of us. My mama would've called her trifling for dancing in panties and see through tights, but I just called that shit a good time. And the way her long signature boots could barely contain the thickness of her thighs was definitely gonna be a problem for me tonight.

"What brings you here, Mr. Smith?" she asked after breaking the embrace that I would have let go on until it started to make everybody in the room uncomfortable.

"I felt like dancing and I heard this was the best class in

town."

"And you just so happened to pick Ladies 'N 'Lettos Night?"

The smirk on her full lips was begging to be nibbled on, but instead I looked around at all the women in stilettos and not much else. There were a few other men sprinkled throughout too, but they were dressed in feminine clothes and had their heels on too so I obviously stuck out like a sore thumb.

She was right though because she had two other classes that I could've came to. Sundays were for the grown and sexy crew and Wednesdays were for the kids. But Fridays, they were for the freaks and what she was most known for so it was a no-brainer which class I would be attending.

"I'll just watch you do your thing then," I suggested innocently, but she wasn't having it.

"No gawkers allowed. If you're staying your feet are moving," she said with authority again and I didn't know why I kept picking up on lowkey dominatrix vibes from her.

I wouldn't even let myself finish the thought though because imagining her smothering me with a mouthful of her dripping wet pussy was what my dreams were made of and I would've been rock hard in seconds. I quickly snapped myself out of it right before she connected her phone to the loud speakers and addressed the class.

"Alright ladies, let's show Mr. Smith how to be a bad bitch!"

A beat dropped and they all instantly rushed to get in formation. I knew immediately to pull off my hoodie and tie my hair back because this was about to be a workout.

For two hours I was in a room surrounded by beautiful women wearing almost nothing but the heels on their feet, but Tempest still managed to command my attention. Like follow the leader my eyes went where she went and there was literally no point in trying to hide it because she liked it.

I had seen her dance enough to know that she was doing certain twists and turns with a little extra flair just for me. I loved how her personality came through in her dancing. How playful she was. Her confidence. Even when she tried to play the background to let others shine, I still zeroed in on her.

It was because some people transformed when they performed then regressed once they stopped. Her energy never changed though since it's who she really was and it made me want to know her. Experience her.

"Loosen up, Theo. You have to tap into your femininity. Move your hips," she instructed because I had been acting like I couldn't do some stuff so she could give me special attention.

She walked over and placed her body in front of mine then wined in the opposite direction to show me how it was meant to be done. That's when I stopped pretending and matched her energy to show her that I could move in sync and keep up with her. It was short-lived though since the second I took my eyes off of our reflection and put them directly on her I missed a step.

"Watch the mirror. Not me," she said as she leaned in so only I could hear then took her position back in the center.

Some dancers thought whipping their hair around was enough to get them by, but it was evident that she had studied the art of dance by how particular she was about each step. And while she incorporated the stripper and trendy stuff because they had their place, I could tell she knew there was more to dance than that.

I especially appreciated her ability to tweak her routines on the spot and add layers depending on the skill level of the class too. She created different moves for the people like me who couldn't do splits or who couldn't get back up fast enough. Instead of a one size fits all approach to dancing she examined bodies to determine which movements were best suited for each individual and the final product ended up looking even better.

By the end of class she had worn me out so when everybody started filing out, I took a seat to catch my breath and wait while she talked to people. She had already given us more than our money's worth, but she stayed behind for a while longer to help a couple students that struggled with some of the more complex stuff.

"What's with the toe thing?" I asked her when she made her way back over to me because she had been really particular about toes being pointed a certain way all class.

"Ten years of ballet. But it was a waste of my parents' money since I have bad feet and I never could get completely turned out."

"Excuse me what?"

"Turnout," she began as she showed me how there was supposed to be something wrong with her feet because of her hip structure. But all I could think of was that turned out or not I wanted those legs wrapped around my head sooner than later.

"You always this tired after physical activities?" she asked suggestively since I still hadn't gotten up from the floor.

"Nah I'm good." I tried to pick myself up but had to take my time because I swore the closer I got to thirty everything just started snapping, crackling and popping.

"You got enough in you to try it one more time? For some reason I think you'll do better without an audience for this one."

I was already sweaty and tired, but if she wanted me to dance then I would dance. I prayed that my deodorant didn't fail me now since she had me right in front of her as I gave it all I had left one more time.

"A little better," she critiqued from her seated position before I pulled her up and told her that it was her turn to show me how again. "No, it's getting late."

"We got time," I told her as I put the music back on then purposely wiped my damp forehead with my shirt so that she could see my abs.

Without much further protest her body started moving

with the beat and I was instantly right back where she had left me before, in pure awe of how limber and talented she was. The sexy dance had been awkward for me to pick up, but on her it looked like it was made for her as she dipped then spun around like a dreidel.

When she reached the end of the routine that she had taught us I expected her to stop, but when I finally stopped watching her body and caught her gaze I saw that she was going going gone. Her body looked possessed as it seemed to move without her permission as it brought itself over to me.

I didn't even remember sitting down again until she had helped herself to the seat with me still in it. Her on my lap again brought on the best feeling of déjà vu only this time my hands weren't restrained and they had no reason to be anyway because we were finally by ourselves.

She didn't object to where I planted them either and instead squeezed her legs around me. I felt her warm breath on my face as she finally showed some signs of breathlessness. I didn't attribute it to the dancing like mine had been though. No she had definitely just been holding hers while she hyped herself up to finally go after what she wanted.

Our lips touched again, hers gripping mine then lightly sucking on them one by one and causing me to moan into her mouth. My mind jumped several steps ahead of us because from that point on all I could see was me on top burrowed deep inside of her while we watched ourselves in the mirrors.

Right when I was about to make the first move to get us there we heard a phone ring on the other side of the room. It was obvious that it wasn't hers or mine since they were both beside us so she stopped or rather tried to stop what we were doing. I for one didn't care who walked in on us because now that I knew for sure that she wanted me too I had a one track mind.

"Wait Theo!" she chuckled into my lips as she had to practically pry herself off of me.

It was a good thing she did too since she was barely up for a second when the door opened and in came a couple of her students. One of them was the guy who had correctly called me out for coming here for Tempest and I saw him looking at her suspiciously for still being in there with me. I pretended to search for something in my bag to look busy while she made plans to go for drinks with them after class the following week.

When I looked up again she had swapped out her heels for sneakers and was jumping into a pair of sweatpants as they left again. Neither one of us said anything about what we had almost been caught doing, but I followed behind her closely just knowing we were leaving together until I saw her on the app about to get an Uber.

"I can take you home," I told her after we were out of the building but before she confirmed a ride.

"It's far," she said obviously choosing to focus on her phone instead of looking at me.

"That's cool. It'll give us a chance to talk about what just happened in there." She chuckled then finally brought her eyes up to mine.

"Nothing happened."

"It was about to."

"No that was just on-stage Tempest again. I told you she gets me in trouble sometimes."

"Oh okay. Was there a stage in there that I didn't see?" I asked sarcastically as I playfully looked around and she burst into laughter. "Wait here," I told her before jogging over to the lot to get my car.

Instead of getting right in

when I pulled back around she leaned down and spoke through the open passenger window. I spied cleavage for the first time all night but made myself focus on her face to seem more trustworthy.

"I have roommates and you have a girlfriend," she said as if that would affect whether or not I took the long drive, but I chose to hear something else.

"You saying if you didn't have roommates you would invite me in then?" That got a smile out of her as she shook her head. "And just for the record that's not my girlfriend. Not anymore."

"It didn't look like that to me," she said neutrally.

"Looks can be deceiving."

"No actually they're usually right on the money. For instance the look on your face tells me all I need to know about you because subtlety is not your strong suit, choirboy."

"What you mean?" I played dumb to throw her off my scent, but it didn't make a difference.

"I mean your eyes have been fixed on my body for hours. I know it's a masterpiece and all, but that cannot be healthy," she said with the same confidence that she danced with.

I liked that she was cocky too

because that humble shit wouldn't have even been believable from her. She knew how bad she was and it didn't make sense to pretend otherwise.

"You've been watching me too though. I counted ten videos of you dancing to my songs. Two that aren't even out yet," I said finally remembering to ask her how she had gotten her hands on them in the first place, but she zipped her lips.

"I'm a fan. Sue me," she dared me, but the way she said it made me think she meant it in the **F**reak **At N**ight kind of way.

"Nah. Just buy me some froyo and we'll call it even," I said before killing the engine then leading her over to the shop next door.

Of course when we got inside I didn't actually let her pay for it, but I did tease her for getting basic vanilla and not loading up on toppings like I did. Instead of heading back over to my car we took a rest in the outdoor seating area and continued our banter.

"And since we're putting stuff on the record, jot down that I'm fresh out of pussy so I hope that's not the only reason you came to my class," she said after slowly pulling the small spoon out of her mouth and I couldn't help but laugh at her bluntness.

Running through her videos I had seen quite a few rappers and singers show up when she danced to their songs and it was always obvious what type of time they were on. Some artists genuinely just went to promote the single, but I figured she had probably put me in the same category as the others so I decided to finally bring out my trump card.

"Nah I came for business purposes only. Couldn't help but admire the view though," I told her honestly to earn some brownie points.

"And what business do you have with me?" she asked curiously while carefully stepping over the last part.

"Well we're definitely doing your routine in the video Sunday so everybody thinks it would be a good look if you were in it too."

"As what? Backup dancer number four for my own shit? I'll pass."

"Actually you'll be my girl. I-I mean my leading lady," I stuttered out then cleared my throat. "I mean that's if you want to be."

"You're doing this for the publicity then? I know records aren't selling like they used to, but I didn't think you did stuff just for clout."

"You think you can help me

move more units than almost dying did?" I asked reminding her of how many records I had sold when people thought I might not make it earlier in the year.

"I helped you be a bad bitch for a night, didn't I?" she quipped before taking in another mouthful. "Theo, do you really want me to be in your video or are you just using it as an opportunity to try to get something else from me?"

"You think a choirboy like me would do something like that?" I asked sarcastically trying to dodge the question because it was almost true in a way.

"Yes because you've probably

been watching all my videos and wrongly assuming that I can bust a split on your dick and ride you like a rodeo. Well guess what? I can't. And I wouldn't even if I could," she said making us both laugh louder than we intended to.

"I don't know why my little stiff twerking be driving y'all menfolk so crazy," she said without any pomp. It was just an observable fact.

"But let me guess. You're *different* and I intrigue you, right?" She was being sarcastic, but it was actually exactly what I had been feeling. I looked over and expected her to show signs of nervousness from being studied, but she didn't.

"Maybe."

"Definitely. But trust me. Don't go chasing waterfalls. Stick to the rivers and lakes that you're used to…and can actually handle," she said cryptically and it made me wonder if she was using a metaphor for her pussy.

"Hold up. Handle you? You don't think I can handle you?"

"I don't think most men can handle what comes with dating me."

"Who said anything about dating?" I asked just to see her reaction and it tripped her up like I expected it to. "I'm playing but trust *me*. I've never not for a split second doubted if I can handle anything about you, Temp. Fuck around and find out. I'mma leave your ass sleep and sucking your thumb like a baby," I said threatening her with a good time.

"But forget all of that…at least for now," I emphasized to let her know it was still on the table. "You gonna do the video for me or what?"

"I don't know. I gotta think about it."

"Okay and while you're pretending to think about that, think about this too. I want you to do the choreo for my new tour."

I hadn't told anybody not even my family about the good

news yet because it was almost too good to be true. To think it wasn't even that long ago that I was still fighting for my life so to be back out here thriving and getting the chance to experience new things and new people was something that I was eternally grateful for.

"Since when are you touring again?"

"Since now. I got the call this morning and they're picking out dates for the fall. All arenas."

"Well that's amazing for you and I appreciate you thinking of me, but I don't tour with male artists anymore," she said before I dug into her reasoning. "You know why. Because all y'all want to do is fuck the dancers."

"That's not always true."

"So you don't want to fuck me, Theo?" she asked with a sneaky smile and a tilted head.

"Whoa whoa whoa. Objection. That's a trick question and you know it," I said playfully.

"That's what I thought. And that's exactly why my black ass will be cozy at home come autumn not on tour with you," she said definitively which made me put my scoop down so I could really focus on convincing her that things actually would be different with me.

"Nah. Look you got it all

wrong. Yes I've been thinking about hitting it from every possible angle since I first saw your video," I said candidly before moving the few locs that had fallen down from her shaking her head at me.

"But what I really want is your dope choreography and beautiful ass on tour making me look good up there regardless. No pressure about anything else. You can decide for yourself if or *when* you want a bunk or the other side of my bed."

# 4
## DIRTY DANCING

*"Quit playing, Theo. Give it to me."*
*"Give me you first."*
*"You mean for the tour, right?"*
*"To start? Yeah."*

It took one full business day for Tempest to get back to me about appearing in my video, but getting her to agree to do my twenty-five city fall tour was a completely different story. Trying to convince her had been some of the most fun I'd had in years though so I wasn't exactly complaining about how difficult she was making it.

"Just say the word and it's yours, Temp," I said teasing her with the four minute MP3 file of a song my fans had been begging me to release for years after a sample leaked.

It was low of me knowing how much she loved my music, but it was the last card I had left so I had been cruelly singing it to her every time we talked on the phone.

"Okay. Alright. Fine. I'll do it. And that song better be in my inbox by the time I get downstairs or I'm not going," she pointlessly threatened because I'd had the email saved in my drafts for days now.

"Yeah yeah. Bring that ass here already. I've been waiting out here for about forty-five minutes."

"It's been every bit of fifteen and it's not my fault you're the only negro not on CP time. Must be your lack of melanin," she cracked because she was blessed with enough for the both of us.

The drive to Vegas usually took me about four hours, but I had a feeling it would take longer than usual with Tempest along for the ride. I made sure to tell her to be ready at dawn since shooting for the video started at noon sharp, but it ended up just being a suggestion at this point.

I was leaned up against my car and getting ready to call her again when she finally walked out of her building like she didn't have a care in the world. It really had been forty-five minutes by then, but I didn't even care because the way she looked made it more than worth the wait.

"You look like you just stepped out of the early two-thousands," I told her before reaching for the black duffel bag on her shoulder. After tossing it in the backseat, I turned back to look again at how well she filled out her fitted velour jogging suit. I was expecting a smile mirroring my own, but her face said that she was already over the day and it had just gotten started.

"Remind me again why we couldn't just fly there," she spat out before I could even ask what the issue was.

"Because I never fly to Vegas. It was where I had my first show that wasn't in LA so I take the drive every time to remember how far I've come."

"That's sweet and all, but I don't know how I feel about being your passenger for too long after how you started the year off," she joked finally letting out a smile as she referred to my accident.

I didn't exactly frown at her words, but I guess my expression changed enough for her to backtrack and quickly apologize.

"It's cool," I told her before finally pulling her on me for a tight hug to forget about it as I closed my eyes and inhaled. She smelled even better than I remembered because now I was picking up the scent directly from her neck instead of her clothes like before.

"Mm mn. Let me go. I thought you were just in such a hurry. What happened?" she asked sarcastically because I had been rushing her.

"Nah. We're good on time. I just wanted to do this for a little bit before we left," I said directly into her skin before kissing the same spot.

"Mm. What did I tell you about doing that?" she asked after a brief moan escaped her lips.

Just the night before she had made me promise to keep everything professional and about the video, but it was a lie I didn't have to tell since by that point I was sure I wanted more than just a cameo from her.

"I don't know. I wasn't listening. I was probably too busy thinking about doing this."

My lips left a trail from her neck up to hers, but right when I was about to connect with them she stopped me. I expected it because even though we had been flirting heavy on the phone for the past couple days, she was still lying to herself about what we would become to each other.

I wasn't a psychic by far, but even without a crystal ball I knew she would be mine soon.

I let her off the hook about the kiss for the time being though because we actually did have to get going and the way traffic was set up I wouldn't have been surprised if we had to go right to set. Usually when I came to Vegas

I would stay a few days to lose some money on the strip and lay up, but this would just be a simple one day shoot out in the desert.

We would be in and out then headed back home in the morning so I planned on making the most of the short road trip time with Tempest. I had big plans for us later that night too, but in the meantime I was focused on getting us there in one piece and getting to know her better.

"So what are you wearing tonight because it don't really look like you got date attire back there?"

"Why would I need date attire when I'm not going on a

date?"

"Because you are tonight with me." I took my eyes off the road for a second to see if she would keep protesting it like she had been for the last couple days, but she actually wasn't paying me any mind.

"Did I finally wear you down?"

"No. I just know you're not gonna stop until we get it over with so let's do it."

"Damn right. And DeeDee already has your sizes so text her to get you what you need. You know a dress, shoes, some sexy panties just in case you want to show 'em to me," I said just to be mannish as I glanced over at her again.

"That won't be happening," she said with a smirk. "I don't really wear panties these days."

"Ay cut that out. That's the type of shit that's gonna make me crash again for real," I said putting my eyes back on the road and my hands at ten and two.

"Oh so you can joke about it, but I can't?"

We had a good laugh over my hypocrisy, but by the time it died down I suddenly felt comfortable enough to unwrap some shit that I'd held close to my chest for months.

"There was nothing actually

wrong with my tires that night, you know? Everybody thought they blew out, but really I had just been drinking a lot at my album release party."

From the corner of my eye I saw her turn to look at me, but she just watched like she was waiting for me to continue. I didn't know what else to say though or why I had even bothered telling her something that Jonathan and the label had worked so hard to cover up.

I was just thankful that nobody but my dumb ass was hurt when I wrapped my new whip around a streetlight on Sunset Boulevard on New Year's

Day. I could've never lived with myself knowing that I had hurt somebody or taken a life.

"Well that was a pretty stupid thing to do," she said sarcastically after too much time passed without any words between us.

"Tell me about it," I told her even though I didn't necessarily regret anything that had happened. Because with a mildly successful first single at the time and a newly released album full of bangers, God must have known that I was about to start getting high off my own supply.

And who knew what trouble I would have gotten myself into

with the current number one I had. But having to learn to walk again and having somebody else wipe my ass until I could do it myself humbled me in record time. I had taken too much for granted before, but now I fully appreciated life and everything I had and could have more than ever.

"I'm glad you're still here, Theo," she said after another moment of silence. "When I heard about your accident I cried more than I should have for somebody I'd never met before."

"You actually cried for real?"

"I did. I thought I would lose my fave before I ever got to tell you how much your music means to me."

I couldn't see her sweet eyes because I was carefully merging onto I-15, but her tone said that her words were sincere even before she leaned over and kissed the side of my face. I gripped the wheel tighter than I needed to when she connected with the corner of my lips a few times.

"I'll give you a real one when we stop," she promised with her hand firmly planted on my leg.

"Shit. I'm about to pull over right now if you don't move your hand," I joked before stealing a quick peck from her.

After getting that off my

chest I decided to let the music speak for me so we had a little concert in the car. Usually I didn't like listening to my own music when other people were around, but I made an exception since my finest fan requested it. And even I had to admit my shit slapped even harder with her in the passenger seat vibing and wining to each track. The four hours flew by in a flash and I hoped that she would have the same effect when we got on tour.

One stop and a couple kisses later we were pulling up to the hotel we would be staying at for the night. I had gone all out and gotten us one of the royal suites so we could be separate but still accessible. I did have a feeling that her side would just be a formality though after how she had let me get a handful when we stopped for coffee and donuts.

DeeDee was fresh from the airport with an attitude to match her dark clothes when she met us in the lobby to take our bags up and get us checked in. I knew what it was about so I ignored her, but I saw what time it was when Tempest asked to borrow my shades in the elevator. I had never seen her annoyed before so I thought it was cute how she couldn't control her face, but I decided to say something before it grew legs.

I had foolishly thought DeeDee's little ungrateful ass would've been happy that I upgraded her flight to first class, but she was still heated because I wouldn't let her drive in with me. To her Vegas had always meant road trip and shopping time for me, her and Nat so I figured she felt slighted when I told her I wanted it to be just me and Tempest this time.

"Cut it out," I told her simply when Tempest went to her side to unpack her bag. "You don't have to like her just 'cause I do, but you don't gotta be mean to her either."

"So you like her?" she asked

like I hadn't just said that I did, but I nodded anyway. "How when you were just so in love with Nat?"

"I haven't been in love with Nat in a long ass time, DeeDee," I told her honestly, but before she could let me elaborate she raised her voice then her body out of her seat.

"Now you don't love Nat?! So you're really choosing this new bitch over the woman who's been there for you through everything? Buying her a fucking Birkin with money you wouldn't even have if it wasn't for Nat," she spat at me and I tried to shush her so she wouldn't ruin the surprise in case Tempest was listening to us.

"First of all watch your mouth because it's about to take you from first class to a Greyhound real quick," I threatened for no reason because she knew how much it took for me to really get upset with her and she wasn't quite there yet.

"Second, I know exactly why I have what I have and if Nat wanted it she would've gotten it in all the years I've been offering it to her. But whatever it's too late for that now and I want somebody else so you need to accept it just like she did."

"She hasn't accepted shit.

She's been on me and Mama's phone every day talking about you and your new bitch," she said to my surprise only I didn't know what she wanted me to do with that information.

"So block her then." I looked down at my watch to check the time. "And you got a lot of work to do today so gon' head and get to it."

"Right. Because on top of everything else that I already have to do for your video, now you want me to go find clothes for you and your 'date' too," she complained on her way out then let the slammed door say goodbye for her.

I just sighed then laid back on the bed hoping to relax for the last few minutes before it was time to leave. My eyes were barely closed for a few seconds when I heard the door from Tempest's side creaking open and that let me know that she really had heard everything.

"Don't even sweat that, alright? It was about me. Not you. She'll warm up to you after a while," I promised before realizing that I was also telling her that I planned on having her around for a while.

"If you say so." My eyes were still closed, but I felt her coming closer then lying down beside me on the bed. I slowly opened them to find her propped up on an elbow and smiling down at me. "You really got me a Birkin, choirboy?"

"Nope. After all it took to track down a real one, I got *me* a Birkin and I'mma be in these streets stuntin' with it all summer long too," I joked as I sat up for a second to bless her lips which she allowed with no hesitation. "Thank you again."

"You're very welcome, but if I would've known you were really gonna buy it I would've asked for a car instead."

"You can have both then. You can have whatever you want

from me, Tempest."

The weighty words didn't register until after I had said them, but I didn't bother taking them back because I meant them. I didn't care if I sounded like a trick or not because she had turned me into a proud one just that fast. I wanted her and I wanted to take care of her too.

"Damn you must really want a piece of this, huh?" she cracked as she lazily ran her nails over the bottom of my stomach.

"Nah. I don't do pieces. I want all of you all the time starting now."

She initiated the kiss that followed, but she obviously didn't expect it to get out of hand so quickly. Before either one of us knew it my body was on top of and aligned with hers and thinking of an excuse for why we would be late soon. Because now that I knew she was down I was no longer opposed to finally being on CP time.

"Mm you can't keep kissing me and talking to me like this unless you're about to be my boyfriend, Theo," she moaned out after finally coming up for air.

"What if I am?"

"Then we have a problem because Hot Girl Summer is right around the corner and I'm not trying to be boo'd up."

"Nah. Cuffing Season came early this year. You're not about to do this to nobody but me," I told her confidently as I began taking off my shirt but a series of heavy thuds hitting my door stopped me before I could get it over my head.

For a second I considered ignoring them and getting back to what Tempest had started, but I recognized the knock as Jonathan's and I knew he wasn't going anywhere until I came out.

"Wait. I don't want anybody to see me in your room," she said just a little too late because I had already opened the door.

"It's just J and he was gonna

find out sooner or later anyway," I said nonchalantly as I stepped back to let him come inside.

"I would find out what sooner or later?" he asked before he spotted her on my bed.

She had sat up and smoothed out her clothes some, but she still looked just as guilty as she did when I had her on her back with her legs spread a second ago.

"Oh yeah. It didn't exactly take Sherlock to figure this one out," he chuckled out before telling her it was nice to see her again.

"You're gonna be seeing a lot more of her too. She finally agreed to come on tour with us."

He nodded along and made more small talk with her while I got everything I would need for the video, but I still sensed uneasy energy coming from him. She didn't pick up on it though so I packed those thoughts away with the rest of my stuff then hit the lights on our way out.

We separated the second we hit the set. She had tried to get an Uber there so it wouldn't look like we came together, but we were already cutting it close with time so I didn't let her. I told her to stop overthinking shit anyway because people were probably already thinking it and it wasn't like it would be a lie anymore.

After I showed her to her trailer, I headed straight for mine since I was tired from all the driving and not getting much sleep the night before. I laid down while they got started with the parts that didn't involve me and told DeeDee not to wake me up a second before it was necessary.

I had thought about staying up and walking Tempest through everything since this was her first lead role in a video, but I knew she was in good hands and didn't need me hovering over her while she did her job. And I had already kind of done that when it came time to pick out her clothes.

It had never even occurred to

me to care about what my video girls wore before, but I had the stylist drop a bag on hers since I specifically wanted her to match me with her white shorts and thigh high boots. It was almost like her signature and I could understand why since they looked so good on her.

When I left my trailer a few hours later, I looked like I had stepped out of an episode of *Miami Vice* with the rolled up sleeves of my white suit jacket, but it was a good look overall. The sun had been Willie Beamen in the window while I slept so I expected it to burn me up the second I came back outside, but the industrial coolers were on and working overtime.

It was still hot but bearable, but what I saw in front of me was what made my body heat up higher than the desert's temperature. The music was turned all the way up and there were people everywhere making sure everything went off without a hitch so I knew I surprised them all when I cut the take that they were working on.

I could watch Tempest dance forever but not when she was off to the side and barely in frame. It obviously bothered her, but she still did her job and shook that little ass like it was going out of style until I told them to stop.

"Ayo Zach, I don't like it. This ain't what I asked for. It's off balance because Tempest was made to be in the center not the back."

The director was already flustered and pink from the sun and it just got worse as he tried to explain that she had been moved around in each spot to add more dimension after editing. I still wasn't feeling it though and I saw it for exactly what it was, an excuse to not have the camera centered on her. And I wasn't having that.

Nobody put Tempest in the corner.

This was exactly what she thought would happen when she first turned down the video so there was no way that I could let it continue without saying something.

"Sorry for wasting everybody's time," I raised my voice so the dancers could hear me from so far back, "but the good news is y'all are still getting paid so don't spend it all in one place," I said playfully and got a few laughs from the camera guys.

Jonathan wasn't amused though I saw as he stomped over and asked to speak to me in private.

"Wait hold up. I'm about to

make Zach give me a co-director credit for my new idea," I said to put him on ice for a minute before pitching the concept. "Let's keep the part with the platform. We'll get me, Tempest and a chair up there, but instead of it going in circles, let's play with the angles and do it with the cameras instead."

"I don't know Theo. That sounds a lot simpler than we previously discussed."

"You obviously haven't seen Tempest in action yet. Let's just try it out first then decide, alright?" I offered as a compromise even though my mind was made up.

He agreed right when Jonathan damn near lost his mind and demanded that I speak to him alone. Before we caused a bigger commotion I followed him over to my trailer because it was clear that he had been behind all the ideas that I'd just axed.

"Theo, what the hell are you doing?!" he yelled before I could even close the door. "We got a lot of money on the line here! You want to fuck the girl? Cool. Go for it. But do it on your own damn time, man. Not on mine!"

I usually had nothing but reverence for Jonathan since he was close to my pop's age and he always treated me like one of his own kids, but it was clearly time to rebel some and remind him that he worked for me and not the other way around.

"A better question is do you want to get paid? 'Cause if you do then you need to just do shit how I say I want it done without tweaking it to your liking. You're the behind the scenes nigga so stay back there and let me worry about what the world sees when they see my name, alright?"

"But--" I cut him off because there was nothing he could say to excuse what he'd done.

"But nothing. We both know you're not about to walk away now that the hard work is over so just sit back, relax and let Tempest keep doing your job. 'Cause it's a mob of managers that would love to get your cut right about now."

"Mr. 'Day Ones Only' is threatening to replace me because of some groupie he just met? That's the craziest shit I've heard in years," he said finally finding the laugh he had misplaced before.

"I'm not threatening shit, J. You decide your own fate. I'm just letting you know how it's gonna be on Team Theo from now on. Get with it or get lost."

I could've easily taken a shot at his wife and how she had

gotten her start in the business back in the day, but I decided not to play in the mud with him since I knew Tempest was anything but a groupie.

For the first time all day it was quiet on set, but everybody was still trying to look busy for some reason even though they obviously didn't know what they were supposed to be doing. I didn't see Tempest around so I went to her trailer to personally tell her the new direction we were going in.

I didn't bother knocking or watching to see if anybody was paying attention to me because I just wanted to make sure she was good after all of that confusion. I found her alone standing over the sink and awkwardly drinking a bottle of water through a long straw then smiled to myself.

"What are you doing?"

"Nothing. I don't want to get dirty or mess up my makeup. Everything is literally perfect."

She wasn't exaggerating either. Her hair and makeup was done up nicely and the clothes looked even better than expected.

"That's what we have extra shit for, Temp. Now sit your ass down. I know your feet are hurting from all that dancing. C'mere," I urged her to take a seat next to me on the couch.

I unzipped her boots one after the other then put both feet in my lap to massage them. I tried to ignore the elephant in the room and pretend like nothing was wrong, but she saw right through it and confronted me about it.

"Is everything okay now with you and Jonathan and the director?"

"Yeah I just had to pull rank and let them know who's the boss around here," I said in a playful way even though I was dead serious.

"Don't tell me you're already acting like a diva?"

"One of us has to. And for real don't let no shit like that

happen again. Closed mouths don't get fed, Temp. If somebody is doing something you didn't agree to then you better make some noise until they get it right. You hear me?"

"I know and I usually do. I just didn't want to cause any static on your set." She forced her eyes down from mine then put them on her cute fat toes. "I know this is big for you, Theo and honestly just being here period is a dream come true."

My heart did the closest thing to smiling that it could do as I pulled her chin up to look me in my eyes. I couldn't believe how lucky I was to have somebody like her already in my corner before we had even formally met. She really was a fan first and just wanted the best for me.

"It's big for both of us. This moment wouldn't have even happened without you, Temp so I'm not about to let it happen *without* you."

# 5
## SAVE THE LAST DANCE

Anybody who said that Tempest had shown all she could do back when she took over my stage would be eating their words when they saw the video because even with no sleeves on she still had a few hidden tricks for us all.

After the first take I knew Zach regretted using the word simple to describe the new idea because his pink turned red face was all smiles along with everybody else's watching her in awe.

 She had killed it then resuscitated it just to murder it again for anybody that had dared to doubt her.

Even Jonathan's bitter ass couldn't deny how dope she looked when we watched some of it back on the screen. That didn't really matter to me though. All I cared about was the big smile on her face that she kept getting whenever she looked down at me.

*"You're making it really hard to be professional, Theo."*

*"Meanwhile you're just making it hard."*

The sun packed its bags and went home long before we did, but at the end of the night I still wasn't ready to call it quits. In fact if everything went according to plan then my real night would just be getting started.

Both Tempest and me were tired from the long day we'd had, her even moreso because she hadn't gotten a nap in like I did. I let her get some sleep on the drive back to the hotel though since there was no way we could leave Vegas without celebrating such a job well done.

Aside from the donuts that morning neither of us had eaten all day so we both got ready in a hurry for our late dinner. With all the noise DeeDee made earlier I half expected her to come back with an ugly dress for Tempest, but lil' sis had done good...real good.

It fit her like a glove and showed off everything that had been making my mouth water for the last few weeks. She obviously liked it too since I found her admiring herself in the mirror and taking selfies when I crossed over to her side of the room. She worked her angles well, but from where I was standing they were all pretty good to me. If it felt even half as good as it looked...

She didn't ask any questions

about where we were going until we pulled up to the Mandalay Hotel to park. She'd assumed we were going to a restaurant inside until I grabbed her hand and brought her over to the House of Blues.

"Why are we here? I thought we were going to eat not see a show."

"It's midnight. The show's been over," I said vaguely before leading her into the building. "But before we leave in the morning I wanted to bring you to my favorite spot in town."

It'd been closed for service an hour before, but that didn't apply to us since I had unofficially reserved it for the night. I knew a guy who knew a guy who arranged the whole setup, but I knew she wouldn't care how I had done it when I heard her actually gasp as we made our way from behind the curtains and onto the mainstage.

"Theo," was all she could get out as she put her hand over her heart.

All the overhead lights were out so it should have been pitch black in there, but there were enough candles lighting up every few seats in the balcony to give us a dim romantic vibe. It went perfectly with the sexy jazz instrumental coming through the speakers.

There was a spiffy table for two and a full serving staff hanging back and waiting for us to start our meal, but for a minute it felt like it was just the two of us in there when I wrapped my arms around her from behind.

"I understood the assignment, right?" I bragged into her neck because the view we had was breathtaking even for me and I knew it was coming.

"Mm you may have done a little homework, choirboy," she said downplaying it before admitting that it had actually crept into extra credit territory.

I released her from my hold

then pulled out her chair because I was ready to slam the delicious steak that I smelled in the air. I still wasn't partaking, but I opened the chilled bottle of wine for her since I didn't want to stop her from enjoying herself just because I wasn't.

When we got to the point in the night that we couldn't eat another bite and there was more talking than chewing, I pulled her seat over to mine so that we could relax for a minute while we looked around at all the lights again.

"Today was really something, wasn't it? I definitely needed something chill like this to end the night. I haven't done anything like this since...shit I don't think I ever did nothing like this before," I said to my own surprise since I couldn't recall anything off the top of my head.

"You famous dudes love using that line."

"What famous dudes you got experience with besides me?" I asked sounding more jealous than I intended to, but I wanted to know. She just smiled as she shook her head and laughed at me.

"Oh you thought you were the first? That's cute but no."

"Anybody who came to your class?" I asked because I had

watched just about all of her videos by now and seen way too many familiar faces. Thankfully she gave me a look that said it should have been an obvious no. "Anybody I collaborated with?"

"Nope."

"Then it's not a problem."

"It's not like it would have been anyway."

"How you figure that?"

She reached over to move a couple locs that had fallen in my face then touched my neck. I felt my pulse increase in record speed and so did she.

"You want me too bad. That's how. Not to mention where we are right now. Face it. I've got your nose wide open, choirboy."

I didn't bother denying it because I couldn't. She was right and I couldn't take it anymore so I stole another kiss instead.

"You really do and because of that I'm not waiting anymore, Temp. This is happening tonight." I knew it was risky telling her instead of asking so I was hoping that it didn't backfire.

I still thought it was worth it though since I had just told her closed mouths didn't get fed and I wanted nothing more than to spend the rest of the night feasting on her.

To my surprise she just shamelessly leaned over and

pulled back my pants to peek in my underwear. It caught me off guard so I looked around to make sure nobody was watching us or how bold she was being.

"Oh so that's where all your melanin went, huh?" she joked until I let my hand creep up the slit in her dress.

Once I was sure the coast was clear I was game for whatever she had in mind in here. We could even go up to the balcony and give this place a real show to remember if she wanted.

"You ready to see what it can do?" I asked getting ready to pounce on my prey, but she put a hand on top of mine to slow me down.

"Mm not yet."

"Why not? Why you tempting me like this, Tempest?" I whispered in her ear then gently bit and kissed the lobe.

"Don't be saying my name like that when this wine has already got me feeling too sexy up in here."

"It's not the wine. I've been sober every time I've been around you and I see it too. That's why you're cuffed now," I said with a smile but noticed that she wouldn't look at me. "What's wrong?"

She started to speak then stopped herself for a minute to

find the words that she was looking for.

"I don't have no more heartbreak left in me, Theo. I literally can't take another one and especially not from my fave. You're like an entire genre of music by yourself so what am I supposed to listen to when I wake up from this dream tomorrow?" she asked implying that what was happening between us wasn't based in reality or built to last.

"If that's all that's stopping you then you don't have nothing to worry about. Just wait 'til I get back to the studio and start writing songs that are about you. I think I'mma call the one about tonight 'Light It Up'."

I could tell she thought I was just feeding her more lines so I extracted my hand from between her legs then made our noses touch.

"I promise your heart is safe with me, Temp. I ain't tryna play with nothing but your pussy."

I thought I might have come off more brash than charming for a second, but apparently it was exactly what she needed to hear because after that she was finally ready to go.

We walked into the hotel hand-in-hand and to the naked eye we probably looked like every other couple who was only there to fuck up their beds. We were a little different though since we had two beds to fuck up, one for now and one for later.

As soon as the elevator doors closed I backed her into a corner then let my hands fall down to squeeze her ass. The way she bit her lip told me she liked it, but she had still tensed up enough to let me know I was going too fast.

"You know we don't *really* have to do this tonight if you're not ready? I don't wanna wait," I told her honestly before connecting our foreheads, "but I will."

Both me and my dick were instantly relieved to see the

mischievous grin form on her lips at the suggestion of us waiting any longer.

"I know you would…but I don't want to wait either. Just go slow until I say so, okay? I want something that makes me feel like your music does. Sexy, adored, special."

"It's already done," I promised as I brought my face down to hers. She laughed at my hair tickling her nose so I knew I would have to get a band to keep it from getting in the way.

I made sure to dim the lights on the way in to set the mood right away. We had seen enough candles for the night so I didn't bother trying to find any and instead headed straight for the bed. She smiled at my eagerness to undress but still took her time torturing me by taking everything off one at a time.

I could tell she wasn't wearing a bra so I impatiently waited to meet her big round, brown nipples when she slid the dress down her body. What I actually saw though was a lot of double-sided tape that stood in the way of me being able to latch on like I wanted to. I went to snatch it off and came close to getting my head knocked off my shoulders when she felt me tugging at it.

"That's not how you take off titty tape, fool."

I apologized as I kissed her nipples through the barrier then laid back and waited for her to go and come back from her side. I knew she was about to baptize my shit so I put a couple pillows behind my head and got into position.

A couple minutes later I looked up to find her fully nude silhouette standing in the open doorway watching me while I watched her. The light from the moon shined in on her and all I could think about was how she wasn't kidding when she had called her body a masterpiece.

I had never seen skin so smooth in my life and I refused to go any longer without feeling it draped all over me. I reached out for her and within one blink of my eyes she was in front of me and saddling up to ride.

I promptly told her to put it in reverse so I could taste it first. I wanted her dripping wet when I pushed my way in and there was no better way to achieve that than letting her get a private meet and greet with my mouth.

The temperature in the room rose the second our warm skin connected, but her mounting my face and putting her pussy within my tongue's reach nearly set my body on fire. She was somehow even more eager than I was though and circled the tip of my dick before I could get my first lick in.

On contact it made me leak and throw my head back so I smacked her ass to make her stop so that I could concentrate on my meal. This was the only time it was appropriate for a man to eat first so she couldn't have any until I was full.

"Not yet. Just get it wet and use your hands for now," I instructed because I wanted to actually get to see myself going in and out of her mouth too.

She was a good girl and

released me with an audible pop but not before letting her saliva drip down the shaft.

For a while there I got lost in her moans while I played patty cake with her pussy, but then I found myself when it got too good and she started squirming around. That's when I locked her legs in place and hoovered her clit, loving that she couldn't do shit but let me suck that tension out of her.

In a rare moment of selfishness I admitted that I didn't care how it felt to her. Or at least I didn't care as much as I did about how it felt to me. Sweet, wet flesh on my tongue was nothing new, but hers was tantalizing in a way I had never experienced before. Luckily she seemed to be enjoying herself just as much as I did though.

Her body suddenly caught the shakes so I knew she was coming even before she started reaching out to hold onto something, anything to gain some composure. All she found was me though and she gripped my dick so tight I thought it could burst while she came in nothing but shivering breaths.

Her mouth was open wide but no sounds came out as she began to roughly grind her pussy on my tongue. She'd just had dinner, but she was clearly still starving for at least one more nut. And seeing her like that, all wild and hungry for the things I made her feel had me ready to bust just from her holding me like she was.

Before I could warn her I had shot off into her hand and taken us both by surprise with my jerking body. I was glad I'd gotten the first one out of the way though since I didn't want to come too fast when I finally got inside of her. I wanted to get comfortable and lounge around in her pussy for as long as she would let me.

"Did I say I was done yet?" I asked rhetorically after yanking her back down on my face since she thought it was cool to just get up without my permission. "Now ride this tongue like you about to do this dick."

And she did it. She rocked my shit back and forth then gave me a nasty little wine when I opened her up with two long, curled fingers. Looking at the way she threw it back on me had me hardening up again already and it didn't hurt that she had started massaging my balls and licking me back to life.

By the time I was fully solid and ready to finally get in there, she was sopping wet just how I liked it and gushing all over my face.

"Damn you got me down here looking like those glazed donuts we had earlier," I joked as I came up for air and she weakly chuckled as her body continued to spasm.

"Mm. My favorite. Let me see."

She quickly dismounted but saddled right up again as she turned to face me. I let her wipe my face clean, but my dick jumped when I realized that she had purposely saved some of her liquid gold to taste off of my lips.

More than ever I wanted to feel the lips on her face again, but the lower set were already crying out for me as she dragged them along my dick.

"Put it in," I growled at her with a mouth full of titty so juicy and satisfying that I didn't even mind the little tape residue that she had missed.

Without skipping a beat she held onto my chest and lifted herself high enough to accommodate the long dick that was about to change her life.

I liked how obedient she was to all of my commands because I loved women to be outspoken with me everywhere but the bed. Off top she understood that in here I was Daddy and whatever I said went.

When I felt her bearing down on me, I knew I should have been reaching for one of the condoms in my bag, but I couldn't make myself stop this moment from happening for another second. And when that velvet, slippery grip sucked me in and cradled my tip, I knew it would be worth whatever consequences that might've followed. YO-fucking-LO.

"So you coming out swinging, huh?" I asked already impressed by how she was sliding down slowly then wiggling and gripping me on her way back up. "Stop playing with it though. Make it disappear," I challenged as

I smacked her ass again just to see the ripples up close.

That was the wrong thing to say though because it was what encouraged this woman to turn into a fucking animal right before my eyes. She held eye contact as she dropped all of that spare ass in my lap and grinded on me the same way she had done at my show.

Until that point it hadn't dawned on me just how long she had been thinking about doing this very thing to me. She'd played hard to get for a while to make me work for it, but really she had been ready and willing since day one and that shit turned me on so much.

"Fuck. Keep this up and we gon' have a problem real soon, Temp," I warned her about the chain reaction from how good she felt, but it just seemed to encourage her even more.

Right after I said it she flexed then squeezed me tighter and that's when I realized that she wanted it. She had been hypnotizing me with her eyes and begging me for it. She didn't want me to finish on her butt or stomach but right in her core where it was meant to be. So that's what I gave her.

An avalanche of emotions buried me when I heard her

moaning out my name and saying some straight up nasty shit in my ear. It made my toes curl up so tight I couldn't even feel them motherfuckers anymore.

I usually saved my shouting for the studio, but the explosive sensation that ran through my body could only come out through a holler. I sounded like a wounded dog as I yelped and gave her all I had to give. If I never came again I couldn't even be mad because I couldn't imagine it ever getting better than that.

"Shit. Temp. I can't--I can't fucking breathe," I barely got out, but she just kept grinding her soft, sticky body into mine. I literally had to make her stop because after the shit she had just done, I was too sensitive for any extra strokes.

She sucked in her bottom lip while she watched me catch my breath, looking like the baddest motherfucker alive up there. All that dancing had done her good because her breathing said she had stamina for days and still wanted some more. Meanwhile I felt like I had just did a two hour show when all I'd really done was move my hips to match hers.

But like any other man who had been fortunate enough to get to experience her, I had just learned a satisfyingly sweet lesson: Tempest Randall didn't get fucked. She did the fucking. And once she had coaxed every drop out of me, she finally got off and headed straight to the bathroom.

"You alright in there, choirboy?" she asked smugly after only a minute of being apart even though it felt like longer.

I could barely hold my damn head up, but I did it when I saw that I had a clear view of her sitting on the toilet with her legs spread so that I could see everything. I had never thought anything was even remotely sexy about piss in any way, but even watching her do that was a sight to see.

I didn't know what kind of weapon she had on her, but that shit was definitely formed against me and prospering like a motherfucker.

"No, I'm not good. I knew you were playing when you said you were trash in bed, but that wrist work was impeccable. Top tier grinding and that grip…" I said before making a chef's kiss sound.

She just laughed at me before finishing up then turning on the shower. For a second it was like my brain wasn't connecting to the rest of my body so I had to force it up to stand in the arch to watch her. I didn't know why, but seeing her wash my essence off had me hardening up again in no time.

I didn't get to full mast though until she looked back at me over her shoulder then used the detachable showerhead on her pussy. I knew it had to be hitting her clit because she bit her lip the same way as she did when I sucked on it.

Against my better judgement seeing that made me want to get in with her and fill her up one more time so I did. Before I could even get over to her she had poked it out then put her hands up on the wall like she was about to be frisked. I chuckled to myself about how thirsty she was to get beat by my nightstick again.

After peeling her wet and well satisfied body from the hard tiled wall, she wrapped it in a towel then suddenly went over to her side of the room. Of course I went right after her to see where she was taking my new little friend.

I watched her put on spray deodorant then grab a long scarf to wrap around her locs, but she opted to stay naked as she climbed into the queen sized bed.

"You're not coming back to sleep with me?"

"No, your bed is all wet now."

"Yeah thanks to that Slip 'N' Slide between your legs," I said sarcastically. "C'mon. I'll put some towels down. I need my king and my pillows to fall asleep."

"So go back over to 'em then. I'm not stopping you," she said through a sleepy yawn as she rolled on her side. I just kissed my teeth then told her to go over some since she was lying diagonally. "Aw. You want to cuddle with me or something?" she teased in a sing-song voice as she made room for me.

"No. I gotta get used to sharing this size bed with you anyway since I'mma be sneaking you in my room on the tour bus."

"I'm grown. If I have to sneak

to do it, it's not for me," she said matter-of-factly.

"You know what I mean." Her lashes fluttered around when she rolled her eyes so I kissed them still. She kept them closed for a few seconds too long though and I knew she was falling asleep on me. "I know I wore you out in there, but damn you're out already? I did want to talk for a little while."

"What else could we possibly have to talk about?" she asked sounding amused because I was obviously more worn out than she was.

"I don't know. Something real for a change. We're grown,

right?" I mocked her.

"I am. You might be a little bit. Now what adult conversation would you like to have over the next few minutes because I'm going to sleep soon?"

"Alright well for one you know I took it off safety and unloaded the clip a couple times so are you on any birth control?" I asked as lightheartedly as possible, but she still tensed up again.

"Um…I'll get a Plan B in the morning just in case, but I don't really need one. I won't be having anybody's baby anytime soon," she said simply enough. I assumed that she knew she wasn't ovulating or something, but the way she said it made me want to dig deeper.

"What do you mean by that?"

"Don't worry about it. Let's just go to sleep. I'm tired," she suggested as she gave her back to me then wrapped her arms around a pillow instead of me like I wanted. I scooted closer to put my arm back around her and the heavy breath she released almost made me feel like a nuisance.

"So I don't know if you know this about me, but I'm kind of a fixer by nature and it kinda sounds like there is something you want to talk about." I reminded her how I had shared the truth about my accident earlier then encouraged her to say whatever was on her mind too.

"Theo, please just leave it alone. I really don't want to get into it right now." I could hear the frustration building in her voice, but something wouldn't let me drop it because I knew she had to have brought it up for a reason.

"Alright it's your call. But is it something that you'll feel comfortable talking about eventually or should I just not bring it up again?"

"Look it's really not that serious. I just can't have kids, okay?" She tried to sound nonchalant, but it was impossible considering the subject matter.

"What do you mean 'you can't'? Like you tried before and you can't?" I asked hoping she elaborated on her own so I wouldn't have to keep pulling it out of her.

"Like I had a really fucking traumatic miscarriage that messed me up inside so I'm gonna need a miracle and a lot of money if I ever want to even try again."

I was speechless for a minute not because I didn't know what I wanted to say but because I knew what I was thinking was majorly putting the cart before the horse and I didn't want to scare her away. I was never good at bottling up even the most inappropriate thoughts though so I eventually said them aloud.

"Well I guess it's a good thing you finally got a nigga with Birkin money then, huh?" I said hoping it would make her smile. It worked, but the movement from her round cheeks made several tears fall down with it before I wiped them away with the pad of my thumb.

"When that time eventually gets here for us, Temp I got you, alright? It'll happen when it's supposed to," I promised her then punctuated my words with a tight squeeze.

I considered bringing up that

I'd lost a baby too to let her know that I could relate to her loss, but I decided to save that for a different conversation because I wanted to keep the focus on her for the time being. And while her tears soaked my chest I thought about the sudden new appreciation that I felt for her body.

Because now I understood that it was meant for more than just a good time. Every scar told her story, every curve had a purpose and she was too immaculate to be scrutinized and reduced to a size on a tag.

My hands trembled as I slowly ran them down so that I

could hold her womb in my hand as I pressed my lips into her temple. We both knew it was too much for the first time, but it was where we had ended up and neither one of us would dare put a stop to it.

"I'm sorry for dropping all of this ugly shit on you," she began as she dried her eyes, but I wouldn't let her go down that road because she had nothing to apologize for. "No I do. This is why I always tell myself to just shut up and dance."

"Why would you tell yourself that?"

"It's like my own version of Hakuna Matata. Whenever I get to feeling like I can't get through something I just stop running my mouth and start moving my feet. It's not perfect, but it hasn't failed me yet."

"Why do you love dancing so much?" I asked because there seemed to be something deeper than her just being good at it. I mean I liked it too and it came naturally to me, but it was really just something to do to put on a good show. She seemed to live and breathe it though.

"Because dancing is the one thing that's literally for everybody. It lives in all of us. Put on a beat anywhere in the world and babies just naturally bounce to it. I get so much joy teaching my kids how to express themselves with their bodies, showing women that it's okay to have a sensual side, and watching my old folks prove that they still got it," she said with a wide smile and a look in her eyes that said she was fondly thinking of the students in her classes.

"And I guess maybe I feel like I have something to prove sometimes. Some people act like I shouldn't be at the level I'm at so I like to keep my foot on their necks while I climb even higher," she said finally sounding like her normal cocky self again.

"What about you? Why do

you love singing so much?" she asked flipping the question on me.

"Because it gets me enough money to bag women like you," I joked even though I really had started singing to impress girls back in the day. "But for real I like how it makes other people feel. My voice is a gift that I don't even think I deserve most days, but as long as I got it I'm gon' use it to make the world feel good."

"And that's why you're my forever fave." She planted a sweet peck on my lips before finally laying her head down on my shoulder.

"You're not just saying that

because I dicked you down good, are you?. I'm really your favorite?" I was clearly fishing for a compliment because all signs pointed to yes from the very beginning.

"In more ways than one now," she said softly while rubbing my face.

Falling asleep should have come easily because of how tired I was and how Tempest had completely worked me over, but I was still up long after she had dozed off in my arms. It had been a while since I'd held somebody all night and it was the first time watching her sleep so I couldn't help kissing her face a few times.

I tried real hard to think of something to complain about, but I couldn't come up with a single thing. For the first time all year I felt really good. Content. Happy even. I smiled when I realized that not only was my stomach full and my balls empty, but I was also lying next to Tempest and smelling just like her. Yeah there was definitely nothing there to complain about so I dropped the thought all together before joining her in a much needed round of sleep.

Her scarf had come off not long after she'd fallen asleep, but I didn't wake her up to fix it because she looked pretty and peaceful with it spread over the pillow like a crown. I finally nudged her awake though after she had rolled over and left me on my side alone.

"Why are you looking at me all goofy like that?" she asked over my loud yawn while she tied the fabric down tighter than before.

"Like what?"

"Like you want to do something stupid because of where we are right now," she alluded to us getting married in Vegas.

"I really wasn't thinking that, but now that you mention it…" I began but caught myself before she really thought I was out of my mind. "Nah this trip has already been one for the books so we gotta save something for the next time we come."

"Lord how did I manage to find the first R&B singer who actually lives his song lyrics?" she asked in a playful way. "You really think because I got you off a few times that we're about to go live happily ever after when we've literally only known each other for like a day, Theo?"

"Yeah well I don't know about you, but it was a pretty good fucking day for me."

"Okay Ice Cube," she said sarcastically. "Didn't you ever

hear you're not supposed to date let alone marry your backup dancer? Ask J-Lo and Britney Spears how well it worked out for them."

"Yeah but that doesn't apply to us. You're not just a dancer, Temp. You're my choreographer too," I told her matter-of-factly and she grinned because I'd found a loophole that could satisfy us both.

When I'd first seen her I had foolishly thought this might be a one-time thing, maybe double back a few times if it was as good as I thought it would be. But now I knew that not only did I need *that* on the regular, I wanted the rest of her too.

And just because we wouldn't be jumping the broom that particular night didn't mean she wasn't the only thing that'd happened to me in Vegas that I knew for sure I didn't want to just stay there.

Before she could get back into another rem cycle, I let my mouth convince her that staying up a little longer would be worth her while as I kissed my way south. All things considered my performance before had been good, but a few hours of sleep had definitely done me some good and made me  unstoppable. And nothing could compare to the feeling of being on top of her for the first time.

After marinating and stewing in its own juices her pussy had a different kind of wetness and I used it to my advantage to keep her coming over and over until she finally tapped out. Seeing her with a damp forehead and legs that couldn't quit shaking was a direct contrast from when she had bested me and I felt proud at how complete she looked while full of me.

My hair fell in her face again, but instead of brushing it aside she used it to pull me in deeper as she used up the last of her energy to grind along underneath me.

"That's right. Keep dancing for me, Temp."

As I erupted I saw my future with her flash before my eyes. I saw us on tour falling deeper and deeper in love in every city we visited. Hell from the looks of it pretty soon they would have to invent a new kind of love just for us because the old shit just wouldn't be enough.

It was too early to know for sure if this would become a forever kind of thing, but that didn't stop me from really hoping that it would. And after taking the long way home in the morning, I knew I would be headed to the studio even though I still hadn't even toured the last album yet.

But Tempest had stirred up so many new feelings and it was about time to see what my new muse was made of. Besides I couldn't wait much longer to finally see her dancing to love songs that were made specifically for her.

*When you're ready*
*For my last name*
*Just say the word*
*'Cause girl I'm game*
*Since the beginning*
*I've been feeling the same*

# SHUT UP AND DANCE

# FOLLOW ME

Thanks for reading! If you don't want to miss out on any updates about future works of mine then find me on all social media platforms as TanSaidWhat, sign up for my mailing list, and join my reading group Turning The Page With Tanzania Glover.

Visit www.tanzaniaglover.com

And if the cover art took your breath away as much as it did mine, check out the talented artists Aaronya Medici! Thank you so much for bringing this couple to life!

# THANK YOUS

I said that I was done writing dissertations to my family and friends in this section so I'll try to keep this brief especially since my love for them has remained the same since the first time I did this. But I do want to say that I feel like the luckiest person in the world to be able to go on this journey with people who genuinely love and care for me. Because of the immense amount of love and support that I receive from them, I get to do the thing I love most in the world and I'm forever grateful for it.